MAX
and the
WON'T GO TO BED
SHOW

Mark Sperring and Sarah Warburton

Scholastic Press · New York

Ladies and gentlemen! Boys and girls!
Hurry, hurry, for the

BEST SHOW ON EARTH!

Tonight for your entertainment and
delight, we proudly present, from all
the way behind the curtain,
the world's youngest magician.
Please put your hands together for...

MAX THE MAGNIFICENT!

DRUMROLL, PLEASE!

Tonight we will see his world-famous
and death-defying
PUTTING OFF BEDTIME FOR
AS LONG AS POSSIBLE SHOW!

For his first trick, Max the Magnificent will make one cup of milk and one whole cookie disappear before our very eyes...

v...e...r...y s...l...o...w...l...y...

A...b...r...a...c...a...d...a...b...r...a!

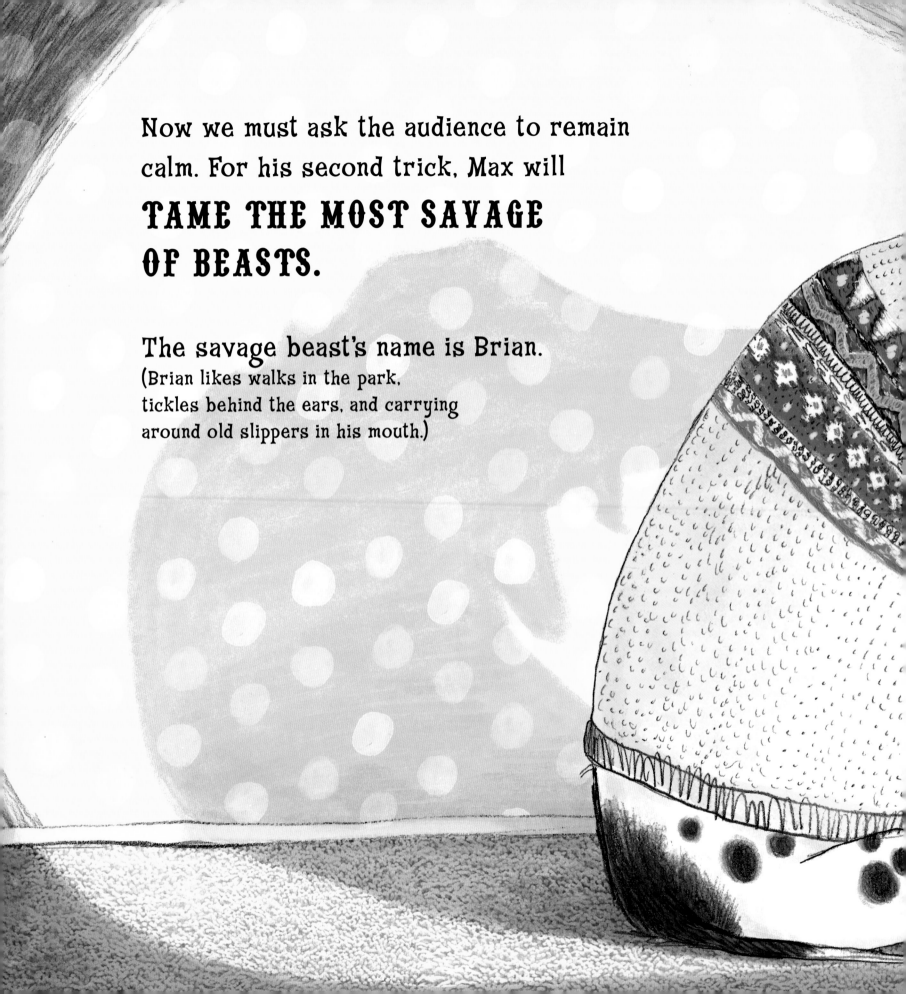

Now we must ask the audience to remain calm. For his second trick, Max will

TAME THE MOST SAVAGE OF BEASTS.

The savage beast's name is Brian.
(Brian likes walks in the park,
tickles behind the ears, and carrying
around old slippers in his mouth.)

YUCK!

That's not fetch!

It's a big, slurpy good-night kiss, and
that can only mean one thing...

...THE GREAT DISAPPEARING BOY TRICK!

Max, where are you?
Is he behind the chair,
ladies and gentlemen?

NO!

Can you find Max, boys and girls?

NO!

Has he vanished in a puff of smoke?

KABOOM!

No, here he is in the bathroom, brushing his teeth!

What a GLitTERing extravaganza!

What a DAzzLing spectacle!

This CERTAINLY deserves a **BIG** round of applause!

And now prepare to be SHOCKED and AMAZED. You are about to witness the seldom seen **FLOATING PAJAMA TRICK.**

Max will cause his pajamas to float off the chair and across the room. And, perhaps the most difficult part of all, he'll attempt to put them on.

Audience, be warned, this trick can take up to half an hour to perform...

...though, luckily, not tonight.

TA-DA!

The show isn't over yet. There are still more thrills to be had...

Max the Magnificent pulls a rabbit from under the bed.

BRAVO!

And a bear from out of the closet.

HURRAH!

And his favorite striped raccoon from out of the toy box.

ENCORE!

Next, as Max the Magnificent crawls
into bed, he will attempt the impossible.

Ladies and gentlemen, boys and girls,
we strongly advise you

NEVER

to try this at home...

Max asks for ten – yes, tEN! – bedtime stories.

(His mom says
she'll read two.)

Now we must dim the lights and ask for quiet. Let's tiptoe out and leave our little magician in peace.

Thank you, ladies and gentlemen. Good night, boys and girls.

Max the Magnificent needs his sleep now. After all...

...who knows what tricks he'll perform tomorrow?

For Harry (Mágico Chico!) – M.S.
Ditto – S.W.

Text copyright © 2014 by Mark Sperring
Illustrations © 2014 by Sarah Warburton

Max and the Won't Go to Bed Show was originally published in the UK by HarperCollins Publishers Ltd.
Library of Congress Cataloging-in-Publication Data Available · ISBN 978-0-545-70822-7
10 9 8 7 6 5 4 3 2 1   14 15 16 17 18 · Printed in China 38 · First US edition, October 2014